Janey and the
Famous Author

Janey and the Famous Author

by Mary Downing Hahn

Illustrated by
Timothy Bush

CLARION BOOKS • New York

For Phil, Ophelia, and Naomi,
of course
—M.D.H.

For David, with love
—T.B.

Clarion Books
a Houghton Mifflin Company imprint
215 Park Avenue South, New York, NY 10003
Text copyright © 2005 by Mary Downing Hahn
Illustrations copyright © 2005 by Timothy Bush

The illustrations were executed in watercolor.
The text was set in 17-point Centaur.

www.houghtonmifflinbooks.com

Printed in Singapore

Library of Congress Cataloging-in-Publication Data
Hahn, Mary Downing.
Janey and the famous author / by Mary Downing Hahn.
p. cm.
Summary: Third-grader Janey is so excited about meeting her favorite author at
a literature festival that she almost ruins the day for her entire class.
ISBN 0-618-35408-5
[1. Authors—Fiction. 2. Books and reading—Fiction.
3. School field trips—Fiction. 4. Festivals—Fiction.] I. Title.
PZ7.H1256Jan 2005
[E]—dc22   2004022051

ISBN-13: 978-0-618-35408-5
ISBN-10: 0-618-35408-5

TWP   10   9   8   7   6   5   4   3   2   1

Contents

1

"I'll Get to Meet Her!"

Today the third grade is studying current events, but, as usual, Janey isn't paying attention. She's reading a Bob the Dog Detective story that she's hidden in her lap. Janey's favorite author, Lily May Appleton, has written many books about Bob the Dog Detective and the mysteries he solves. In this one, he's hot on the trail of a runaway kitten. Bob the Dog is smart and brave. Janey knows he'll find that kitten.

Suddenly, Ms. Lindsay says something that catches Janey's attention. Did she just mention Lily May Appleton's name?

Janey looks up from her book. To her surprise, the other boys and girls have put away their current-events folders. Ms. Lindsay is now talking about a field trip. Quickly, Janey slides her book and her folder into her desk and gives Ms. Lindsay her full attention.

"We'll go to the Literature Festival by bus," Ms. Lindsay is saying. "It's a long ride to the college, so we'll need to leave at six in the morning to arrive on time."

As Ms. Lindsay begins to hand out permission slips, Janey turns to her friend Caroline. "What did Ms. Lindsay just say about Lily May Appleton?" she whispers.

"She's one of the authors we'll meet at the Literature Festival," Caroline whispers back.

"Really?" Janey gasps so loudly that Ms. Lindsay looks at her.

"If you'd been paying attention, Janey, you would have heard what I told the class," Ms. Lindsay says.

Janey feels her face turn red. "Yes, ma'am," she says.

As soon as school is out, Janey runs all the way home to show her mother the permission slip. Janey is so excited she can hardly talk. She hops up and down, and waves *Bob the Dog Detective and the Mystery of the Runaway Kitten* in her mother's face.

"Guess what? Guess what?" she shouts. "We're going to a Literature Festival at Wakefield State College, and Lily May Appleton will be there. I'll get to meet her! She'll sign all my Bob the Dog Detective books!"

"Oh, dear," Mother says. "She'll have a very tired hand if all the children bring as many Bob the Dog books as you."

"Nobody owns more Bob the Dog Detective books than I do," Janey says proudly. "And nobody loves Lily May Appleton's books more than I do. In fact, I'm her number one fan in the whole wide world."

The days before the festival pass slowly, the way they do before birthdays and Christmas. But at last it's the night before the big event. Janey is so excited she can't go to sleep. What will Lily May Appleton be like? Will she bring Bob the Dog Detective with her?

After Janey finally falls asleep, she dreams about Lily May Appleton. She's young and pretty and sweet. When Janey tells her she's her favorite author, Lily May Appleton hugs her and says Janey is her favorite reader. Bob the Dog Detective kisses Janey on the nose and puts his paw print on all her books. It's the best dream Janey has ever had.

Off to the Festival

At five in the morning, Mother wakes Janey and helps her get ready. Then she drives her to school before Father gets up.

It's still dark. Janey can see the moon. She has never been up this early. She's surprised to see so many lit windows.

At school, Mother makes sure Janey has everything—her lunch, her book money, and her big bag of Bob the Dog Detective books.

Janey is wearing her favorite yellow T-shirt. It has a picture of a dog on it. He looks like Bob. All the other children are wearing their special T-shirts, the bright red ones that say OAKVIEW ELEMENTARY SCHOOL on the front.

Janey holds her bag of books close to her chest, but Ms. Lindsay stops her on the bus steps. "Where is your school shirt?" she asks.

"I forgot," Janey says. This isn't exactly true. Janey wants Lily May Appleton to notice her. Her yellow shirt will stand out among all the red ones.

"Oh, Janey," Ms. Lindsay says. "Can't you ever follow directions?"

Behind Janey, someone pushes, someone shoves. Janey is holding up the line.

Ms. Lindsay hangs a big nametag around Janey's neck. "For heaven's sake, don't lose this," she says a little sharply.

Janey hauls her bag of books onto the bus. "Sit here, Janey!" Caroline calls. "I can't wait to see Alicia Harrison Swann! Her books are so funny. They're the best I've ever read."

"They're okay," Janey says, "but Bob the Dog Detective is better. I love the way he solves mysteries."

Caroline looks at Janey's bulging shopping bag. "How many books do you have in there anyway?"

"Thirteen. Every single one Lily May Appleton has written, except the brand-new one." Janey takes a deep breath and lets it out in a rush of words. "It's called *Bob the Dog Detective and the Stolen Necklace.* And I'm buying it today!"

Richard leans over Janey's shoulder. Of all the boys in Janey's class, he's the one who teases her the most. "Lily May Appleton won't sign all those books," he says. "Her hand will fall off."

"Yes, she will!" Janey glares at Richard. He makes her so cross. Why did he have to sit right behind her anyway? He could have sat in the back, far away from her and Caroline.

"Those dog stories are kid stuff," Richard continues. "They aren't even scary. You should read Alfred Underhill's books. He's the only one I want to see today. All the other authors write boring books."

Richard's friend John says, "Janey's a scaredy cat. I bet she's afraid to read Alfred Underhill's books." He thrusts one between Janey and Caroline. It's called *The Creeping Green Slime.* The cover shows people coming out of a graveyard dripping with green gloppy stuff.

"Oooh, gross!" Caroline says.

Janey pushes the book away. John pushes it back. When Caroline tries to grab it, Richard whacks Janey on the head with another Alfred Underhill book. Luckily, it's a paperback and not very thick, but Janey shouts, "Ow!"

Ms. Lindsay stands up and looks at the four of them. "Richard and John," she says, "remember what I told you. If you can't behave, one of you will sit up front with me."

"We weren't doing anything," Richard says.

Ms. Lindsay raises one eyebrow, and the two boys slump down in their seats. Neither wants to sit with Ms. Lindsay.

Finally, the bus pulls into a parking lot on the Wakefield State College campus. Janey stares out the window. She's never seen so many school buses or so many children. Some groups wear green shirts, some yellow, some blue, and some red, like Janey's class. No matter what color shirt they wear, they all have nametags hanging around their necks or pinned to their clothes. Janey touches her nametag to make sure it's still there.

Ms. Lindsay stands up in front of the bus. "We're going to the book sale first. We will have exactly thirty minutes there. Please meet back here at the bus at—" She pauses and checks her watch. "Eight forty-five. Our first session, with Alfred Underhill, begins at nine o'clock."

"When will we see Lily May Appleton?" Janey asks.

Ms. Lindsay looks at her schedule. "Alicia Harrison Swann is second. Then we have lunch. After that we see Herbert Randall. Lily May Appleton is our last author."

Janey groans. So long to wait!

Once they reach the gym, where the book sale is being held, most of Janey's class runs to Alfred Underhill's book display. Caroline heads for Alicia Harrison Swann's books, and Janey

makes her way through the crowds of kids to find Lily May Appleton's books. The table is piled high with Bob the Dog Detective stories. Janey tries to get through the kids surrounding the table, but the bigger ones push her aside. They step on her feet, they bump into her, they get in front of her. Her bag of books is in the way. Janey catches a glimpse of the new Bob the Detective book, but she can't get her hands on it.

"Excuse me," she says, but the big kid in front of her says, "I was here first. Wait your turn."

Janey *has* to have that book. She dodges to the side and tries to push between two boys. "Watch it, kid," says the one wearing the red hat.

Janey runs around to the other side of the table, but no one lets her near the books there, either. Her bag starts to tear and she steps back, afraid of losing her old books. She's about to cry.

Suddenly, a bell rings. As the other children surge toward the exit, Janey grabs the last copy of *Bob the Dog Detective and the Stolen Necklace*. She runs across the empty gym and thrusts her money at the lady behind the cash register.

The lady gives Janey her change and her receipt. "Hurry," she says, "or you'll miss your first author."

3

Where Is Janey's Class?

Clutching her new book, Janey dashes out of the gym. Ms. Lindsay and all the kids are waiting by the bus. No one smiles at her.

"Really, Janey," Ms. Lindsay says tartly. "Can't you ever do as you're told?"

Turning to the other students, Ms. Lindsay says, "Let's hurry. We don't want to be late for Alfred Underhill's talk."

As the children follow Ms. Lindsay across the campus, John tugs Janey's hair just hard enough to hurt. "You made us late on purpose because you don't like Alfred Underhill."

"I did not!" Janey glares at John. "There was a big crowd at Lily May Appleton's table."

"Well, there was an even bigger crowd at Alfred Underhill's table," John says. "Everyone in our class has one of his books, except you and Caroline."

"Sissy baby," Richard says.

Before Janey can defend herself, they enter a building and hurry down a hall to a huge room. It's packed with kids. On the stage is a pudgy man wearing eyeglasses and a tweed jacket. He has rosy cheeks and white hair. He reminds Janey of her grandfather.

"That can't be Alfred Underhill," John says.

But John is wrong. A college student introduces the man. "Boys and girls, I'm excited to introduce a real live author— Mr. Alfred Underhill! Please give him a warm welcome."

Though Alfred Underhill certainly doesn't look like a man who writes scary stories, the kids packed into the room cheer and clap. Dozens of cameras flash.

Soon Alfred Underhill is talking about his stories. Janey shrinks down in her seat and tries not to listen. Then she remembers her new Bob the Dog Detective book. She opens it and begins to read. Before long she no longer hears Alfred Underhill.

When Alfred Underhill finishes his speech, everyone cheers and claps even louder than before. Hundreds of children line up to wait for him to sign his name in their books. They jostle and push each other, they giggle, they talk. The noise is deafening, but Janey goes on reading as if she's sitting in a quiet library.

"Janey," Ms. Lindsay says, "please put that book down. It's time for the next session!"

Janey follows her class to another building and another big room crowded with noisy kids. Alicia Harrison Swann is a jolly woman who looks just like the pictures on her book covers. She talks about writing and how she draws pictures for her stories. She shows slides of her studio and her cozy little house in Maine. She tells funny stories that make everyone laugh, even the teachers.

Janey actually listens to what Alicia Harrison Swann says. She loves to draw almost as much as she loves to read. She thinks she might grow up to be a writer and illustrator of picture books. It sounds like fun.

When kids line up to have their books signed, Caroline says, "You should have bought one of her books."

"I only had enough money to buy *Bob the Dog Detective and the Stolen Necklace*," Janey says.

"That's too bad," Caroline says. "I'll let you read mine after I read them." Caroline has three books, including *The Little Dragon and the Big Bad Princess*, Alicia Harrison Swann's newest book, the one she talked about the most.

Janey waits in line while Caroline and the other children have their books signed. Alicia Harrison Swann signs a piece of paper for Janey. She even sketches a funny pig on it. Janey promises she'll buy *The Little Dragon and the Big Bad Princess* and paste the autograph in it.

After the children leave the building, Janey's class sits on the grass and eats lunch. When they finish, Ms. Lindsay tells them to run and play. Carlos and William start a game of tag. John and Richard climb on a statue. Caroline and some of the other girls toss a ball back and forth, but Janey reads her book.

At one o'clock, Ms. Lindsay calls them together for the next session. She has to call Janey twice. When Janey is reading, she never hears anything.

"Janey always makes us late," Chen says.

"Bookworm!" Richard yells at Janey. John echoes Richard. Soon all the boys are calling Janey a bookworm.

If Janey were a worm, she'd crawl into her book and stay there.

"That's enough," Ms. Lindsay tells the boys as they head into the meeting room.

This time the author is Herbert Randall. He writes science books. Secretly, Janey finds science boring. She likes made-up stories much better. While Herbert Randall describes his meth-

ods of research, Janey sits in the back of the room and reads her book. Bob the Dog Detective is sneaking up the stairs in a dark house, hoping to find the rich lady's necklace hidden in Rodney Crow's room. Janey holds her breath, fearful of what might happen if Rodney Crow comes home and finds Bob the Dog Detective in his room.

Janey reads and reads, on and on, till she finishes her book. Bob the Dog Detective receives a big reward from the rich lady and Rodney Crow goes to jail. Janey smiles. The ending is just right.

At last it's time to meet Lily May Appleton! Janey closes her book and looks around.

Where are her classmates? Where is Ms. Lindsay? The room is full of strangers. She doesn't see red shirts anywhere. The college student who introduced Herbert Randall to Janey's class is introducing him again. The fourth session has started, and Janey is missing her chance to meet Lily May Appleton!

4

"You're Not Lily May Appleton"

Janey slides out of her seat and makes her way toward the exit, lugging her heavy bag of books. She steps on a big girl's foot, and the girl scowls at her. She bumps a teacher with her bag, and the teacher frowns at her. Janey wishes she could shrink to the size of a mouse.

Outside at last, Janey expects to see her class waiting for her. But the campus is empty. Everyone is in the fourth session. If only Janey knew which building to go to. Why hadn't she paid attention to Ms. Lindsay?

Janey runs into the first building she sees. She looks in every room, but she doesn't see her class. She runs to the next building. And the next. Her bag of books grows heavier and heavier. The cord handle cuts into her fingers. Her shoulder aches.

Before long she realizes she's lost. She doesn't even know

where the buses are. Has Ms. Lindsay forgotten all about her? Will everyone get on the bus and go home and leave her here?

Janey sits on a bench and starts to cry. She's lost and she's missed seeing her favorite author. This is the worst day of her whole life. She doesn't know what to do or where to go. And there's no one to ask.

After a while, Janey sees children coming out of the different buildings. The fourth session is over. In fact, the festival is over. Everyone is going home.

Janey jumps up and runs after the groups of children. Her book bag is heavier than ever. It thumps against her legs. She searches for Ms. Lindsay's dark hair. She searches for Caroline, for Tony and Shayla, for Chen and Carlos, for Thomas, William, Maria, Susan, Jen—anyone in her class, anyone at all. Even Richard and John.

She sees yellow shirts, purple shirts, and green shirts, but no red shirts. Not a single one.

Janey is lost in a crowd of strangers, who are laughing and talking to each other. The teachers are too busy rounding up their own students to notice her. No one sees she's crying. No one asks her if she needs help.

Finally, Janey finds another bench. She sits down and cries

and cries. She wants her teacher, she wants her mother, she wants her father. She wishes she hadn't even come to the festival.

"What's the matter?" someone asks. "Are you lost?"

Janey looks up. A woman is standing beside the bench, smiling down at her. She looks kind, but Janey knows all about

strangers. She shouldn't talk to this woman. She wipes her eyes and her nose, but she doesn't say anything.

The woman reads Janey's nametag. "Well, Janey Blake, you must be here for the festival," she says.

Janey gulps and nods her head.

The woman sits down beside her. "Do you mind if I share your bench? I've been on my feet all day and I'm tired."

Janey slides over to give the woman more room.

The woman smiles at her. "Have you lost your teacher?"

Janey begins to cry again. Soon she finds herself telling the woman her story. "I was reading while Herbert Randall talked about science, and when I finished my book, a whole new group was in the room and the fourth session had started and my class was gone. And I couldn't find them. I've looked and looked. I think they went home without me." Janey cries harder than ever.

"Is this the book you were reading?" The woman points at *Bob the Dog Detective and the Stolen Necklace.*

"Yes," Janey wails. "Lily May Appleton is my favorite author in the whole wide world. I've read every single Bob the Dog Detective book. I came to the festival just to meet her, and now I'm lost and I didn't get to tell her I'm her number one fan and she didn't sign any of my books."

The woman pats Janey's hand. "Don't cry. I'll sign your books and then we'll find your teacher."

Janey stares at the woman. "I don't want you to sign my books. You're not Lily May Appleton."

"I guess I forgot to introduce myself." The woman laughs. "I'm Lily May Appleton. Truly I am."

LILY MAY APPLETON

5

A T-Shirt for the Author

The woman can't fool Janey. She's seen Lily May Appleton's picture on the back of many of her Bob the Dog Detective books. She's young and pretty. Her hair is long and dark. She wears fashionable clothes.

This woman is much too old to be Lily May Appleton. And too ordinary. Her hair is short and gray. She's dressed more like a teacher than a famous author.

Keeping a tight hold on her new book, Janey rummages through her bag of books. Finally, she finds one with the picture of Lily May Appleton on it. Silently she reads what it says underneath: "Lily May Appleton lives in New York City with her dog Bob and two cats, Ming and Mo. When she isn't writing, she likes to walk in Central Park with Bob. She gets many of her story ideas from the people she sees there."

Janey holds up her book. "You don't look a bit like Lily May Appleton."

The woman laughs. "Oh, my. That's an old photo. I keep meaning to have a new one taken, but I always forget."

Janey is not convinced. "Where do you live?"

"In New York City," the woman says.

"Who lives with you?"

"My cat."

"Wrong." Janey points at the cover flap. "Lily May Appleton lives with Bob the dog and *two* cats, Ming and Mo."

A sad look crosses the woman's face. "I'm afraid Bob the dog died last year, Janey. Ming died three years ago. Mo is all I have now. And he's sixteen, old for a cat."

"Bob the dog can't be dead!" Janey begins to cry again. "He's still solving cases." She waves her brand-new book at the woman.

The woman puts her arm around Janey. "That's what I love about being a writer. In my stories, I can imagine Bob the Dog Detective going on forever and forever, solving cases just like he always has."

While Janey thinks about this, Lily May Appleton adds, "By the way, I love your shirt. That dog looks just like Bob."

"That's why I wore it today," Janey says, still not sure the woman is who she says she is. "We were all supposed to wear red shirts with our school's name on them, but I just knew that you—I mean, Lily May Appleton—would like this shirt better."

"You're right, Janey. In fact, I wish I had one like it."

Just then someone shouts, "Look! There's Janey!"

It's Caroline.

"And she's with Lily May Appleton!" Shayla shouts.

Caroline runs toward Janey. Shayla and the rest of the class are right behind, all in their red shirts. Their nametags flap in the breeze. Way back, Ms. Lindsay huffs and puffs along. She looks cross.

Janey turns to the woman, awestruck. "You really *are* Lily May Appleton!"

Ms. Appleton nods her head. "Now would you like me to sign your books?"

"All of them?" Janey looks at her bag doubtfully. "Won't your hand get sore from so much writing?"

Ms. Appleton smiles. "I'd be happy to sign each and every one."

The other children gather around to watch Lily May Appleton sign Janey's books.

"Janey's your number one fan," Caroline tells Ms. Appleton.

"She reads your books over and over again," Shayla adds.

After Ms. Appleton signs the last book, Janey says, "I'm sorry I didn't believe you were Lily May Appleton."

Ms. Appleton laughs. "I'll be sure to send my editor a new photograph," she says.

Janey throws her arms around Lily May Appleton and gives her a big hug. "Thank you for signing all my books!"

"It was my pleasure," Ms. Appleton says. "After all, you're my number one fan."

Lily May Appleton walks across the campus with Janey and her class. She chats with them about her cat and her apartment in New York. She watches them scramble aboard the bus. Janey is the last to get on.

Before the bus pulls away, Janey looks out a window and waves to Lily May Appleton. So do the other children, even Richard and John. They wave and shout goodbye until the bus turns a corner and they can no longer see her.

Janey sits beside Caroline. "Lily May Appleton will always be my favorite author," she tells her friend. "But now I have a second favorite author. Alicia Harrison Swann."

Caroline grins. "Guess what? My second favorite author is Lily May Appleton."

Richard pokes his book over Janey's shoulder and waves it in her face. "Well, my one and only favorite author is still Alfred Underhill."

"Mine, too," John says.

Janey leans back in her seat, tired but happy. When she gets

home, she'll go to bed. Snug and warm under the covers, she'll read *Bob the Dog Detective and the Stolen Necklace* all over again.

And the next day she'll go shopping with her mother to buy something special for Lily May Appleton—a yellow T-shirt with a dog on the front.